THIS BOOK

BELONGS TO:

....

....

THE STORY OF
*A Fierce Bad
Rabbit*

THE STORY OF
A FIERCE BAD RABBIT

BY

BEATRIX POTTER

FREDERICK WARNE

FREDERICK WARNE

Published by the Penguin Group
Penguin Books Ltd, 80 Strand, London WC2R ORL, England
Penguin Putnam Inc., 375 Hudson Street, New York, New York 10014, USA
Penguin Books Australia Ltd, 250 Camberwell Road, Camberwell, Victoria 3124, Australia
Penguin Books Canada Ltd, 10 Alcorn Avenue, Toronto, Ontario, Canada M4V 3B2
Penguin Books India (P) Ltd, 11 Community Centre,
Panchsheel Park, New Delhi 110 017, India
Penguin Books (NZ) Ltd, Cnr Rosedale and Airborne Roads,
Albany, Auckland, New Zealand
Penguin Books (South Africa) (Pty) Ltd, PO Box 9, Parklands 2121, South Africa

Penguin Books Ltd, Registered Offices: 80 Strand, London WC2R ORL, England

Web site at: www.peterrabbit.com

First published by Frederick Warne 1906
This edition with reset text and new reproductions of Beatrix Potter's
illustrations first published 2002

Colour reproduction by
EAE Creative Colour Ltd, Norwich
Printed and bound in Italy

THIS IS A FIERCE BAD RABBIT; look at his savage whiskers, and his claws and his turned-up tail.

THIS is a nice gentle Rabbit. His mother has given him a carrot.

THE bad Rabbit would like some carrot.

HE doesn't say "Please." He takes it!

AND he scratches the good
Rabbit very badly.

THE good Rabbit creeps away,
and hides in a hole. It feels sad.

THIS is a man with a gun.

HE sees something sitting on a bench. He thinks it is a very funny bird!

HE comes creeping up behind the trees.

AND then he shoots — BANG!

THIS is what happens—

BUT this is all he finds on the bench, when he rushes up with his gun.

THE good Rabbit peeps out of
its hole,

AND it sees the bad Rabbit tearing past — without any tail or whiskers!

THE END